MADDIE'S PET PEEVE

By Kelli Hicks

Illustrated by Tatio Viana

Rourke
Educational Media
rourkeeducationalmedia.com

www.rourkeeducationalmedia.com

Edited by: Keli Sipperley
Cover layout by: Jennifer Thomas
Interior layout by: Rhea Magaro
Cover and Interior Illustrations by: Tatio Viana

Library of Congress PCN Data

Maddie's Pet Peeve / Kelli Hicks
(Rourke's Beginning Chapter Books)
ISBN (hard cover)(alk. paper) 978-1-63430-372-9
ISBN (soft cover) 978-1-63430-472-6
ISBN (e-Book) 978-1-63430-568-6
Library of Congress Control Number: 2015933729

Printed in the United States of America,
North Mankato, Minnesota

Dear Parents and Teachers:

Realistic fiction is ideal for readers transitioning from picture books to chapter books. In Rourke's Beginning Chapter Books, young readers will meet characters that are just like them. They will be drawn in by the familiar settings of school and home and the familiar themes of sports, friendship, feelings, and family. Young readers will relate to the characters as they experience the ups and downs of growing up. At this level, making connections with characters is key to developing reading comprehension.

Rourke's Beginning Chapter Books offer simple narratives organized into short chapters with some illustrations to support transitional readers. The short, simple sentences help readers build the needed stamina to conquer longer chapter books.

Whether young readers are reading the books independently or you are reading with them, engaging with them after they have read the book is still important. We've included several activities at the end of each book to make this both fun and educational.

By exposing young readers to beginning chapter books, you are setting them up to succeed in reading!

Enjoy,
Rourke Educational Media

Table of Contents

Chapter 1
The Walk Home

Maddie skipped down the sidewalk, humming to herself. Her brown ponytail swung from side to side and her shoes made a swishing sound as they moved along the sidewalk. She loved the walk home from the bus stop after school because she could see so many animals along the way. Maddie loved animals!

Maddie's neighbors, the Smith family, had two cats that liked to play in the yard. Maddie tiptoed as she passed by the house. She squatted down and looked into the bushes in the front yard. She spied the cats hiding under the leaves and watched as the cats' tails moved back and forth in short, quick swipes. Each front paw lifted up and down like they were trying to push a button.

Then, suddenly, the cats sprang from their hiding spot and pounced. Sometimes they targeted a bird and sometimes a squirrel. They even pounced on a toy left outside by the kids on accident. Maddie never saw the cats catch any animals, but she did see them grab a toy sometimes before they turned and took off to a new hiding place.

A tall tree stood in front of the Hernandez family's house and in that tree Maddie saw twigs, leaves, and even some string. Taking a closer look, Maddie saw that those things made a nest and that nest belonged to a family of birds. Maddie listened as the birds called or sang and it always made her smile. Squirrels scampered, dogs barked, and fish swam in the pond at the end of the block. It made Maddie think.

She always wanted an animal of her own. She had a little sister named Chloe, but her sister wouldn't fetch a ball or go for a walk on a leash. She had an older brother named Alex, but he wouldn't follow her commands, or sing, or even swim for her. A pet was the answer. Maddie's parents thought a pet was a good idea and agreed that Maddie was responsible enough to take care of an animal of her own.

Unfortunately, Maddie didn't know what pet would be best for her.

Chapter 2
Talking to Friends and Family

"Get a dog," Maddie's friend Charlie said at school one day. "They lick you, and chase a ball, and you can take them for walks."

"No, No, No," her friend Ebony said. "Anybody can have a dog for a pet. You should get a pig."

"A pig? No way," Irene said. "Pigs are dirty and oink, oink, oink all the time. An ant farm is the way to go. They stay in a plastic house and you can watch them dig tunnels in the dirt. It is so cool!"

Maddie thought and thought. She could not decide what pet would be best for her. A giraffe? Worms?

Maddie was confused, so she decided to talk to her brother. He was in the third grade, so he knew a lot about a lot of things.

Maybe he could help.

"Alex, what pet would you get if you could?" Maddie's brother looked at her, but didn't answer right away. He looked like he was deep in thought. The clock ticked, but Alex still didn't answer.

"Alex," she said, louder this time, "what pet would you get?" Still, he just looked at her. Finally, after a very long time, he responded.

"Why do you need a pet? You can just put a leash on Chloe and take her for a walk." Then, he laughed loudly. He slapped his knee and shook his head, then went back to the puzzle he was working on.

Maddie sighed. She looked around the house trying to get an idea. She saw a glass bowl in the corner, a pile of broken crayons, some plastic strings that looked like grass, a smelly sock, and a box of fish-shaped crackers. She also saw Chloe, who was trying to stand on her head.

"What are you doing?" upside-down Chloe asked her.

"I want to get a pet, so I'm thinking about what to get," Maddie explained. Maddie didn't think her little sister would be much help because she was only four, but Chloe surprised her.

"Why don't you ask a professional?" Chloe said, turning herself upright again.

Hmmm, Maddie thought. A professional who knows about pets. That is brilliant! Maddie decided she would write a letter to a veterinarian to see if she could get some advice. She went to her desk drawer and found a clean piece of writing paper and a sharp pencil.

Chapter 3
Consulting a Professional

Maddie's mom helped her find the name and address of a veterinarian that worked near their neighborhood. Then Maddie wrote a letter.

Dear Dr. Hanson,

I am writing to you about a very important matter. I would like to get a pet, but I can't decide what to get. I was hoping you could help. My house is pretty big, so I was thinking a large animal might be nice. I also have a big bag of peppermint candy so my pet will have something to eat. Do you think a hippo might make a good pet?

Your friend,
Maddie

Maddie put the letter in an envelope and wrote Dr. Hanson's name and address on the front. She put a stamp in the corner of the envelope, walked the letter to the mailbox and slipped the letter into the box. She raised the red flag on the side of the box to let the mailman know she had important mail waiting to be delivered. Now she just had to wait.

Every day when Maddie walked home past the animals, she walked to the mailbox to check for a response from the veterinarian. Finally, after five days, Maddie took a deep breath and opened the mailbox. Maddie was thrilled to discover that inside the mailbox was a letter from the veterinarian. Maddie was so excited that she could hardly stand it. She carefully opened the letter and read what was inside.

Dear Dr. Hanson,

Dear Maddie,

I am so glad you contacted me. We have so much to talk about. I am happy to help you decide on a pet and hopefully I can give you some good advice. Although a hippo is a wonderful and very large animal, they don't live near or with people. They live in water and like to live in a group with other hippos. So even if your house is large, it probably wouldn't be a good choice. I also know a lot about what pets eat, and I don't know any pets that eat candy. Some animals eat meat and some like plants. A pet store would be the best place to get food for your animal. Have you thought about getting a cat?

Sincerely yours,
Dr. Hanson
Your neighborhood veterinarian

Maddie read the letter several times. It did make sense that a hippo was too large and that candy might not be the best dinner for a pet. Besides, the candy belonged to Alex and he probably wouldn't want to share it anyway.

A cat? Maddie sat on the couch and twisted her hair around her fingers while she thought. A cat...a cat? After much face scrunching and head scratching, Maddie decided that it was an excellent idea. A lion or a tiger would be a great pet! She didn't know anyone who had such an unusual animal. She decided to write another letter.

Dear Dr. Hanson,

Thank you for your good advice. A cat is a great choice. I have decided I am going to get a lion. A lion has such beautiful fluffy hair around its face. It would be so much fun to put

braids or ponytails in the lion's hair.
I have bunk beds, so the lion could
sleep on the bottom. I looked in a book
and read that lions eat meat. My mom
makes pork chops and hamburgers for
dinner sometimes so I will share with
my lion. Thanks again for your help.

Your friend,
Maddie

Once again, Maddie carefully folded the
letter and put it in the envelope. She wrote
the name and address of the veterinarian
on the envelope and added the stamp. She
walked the letter down to the end of the
driveway and put it in the mailbox. She
raised the red flag on the side of the box so
the mail carrier would know the letter was
ready to be delivered.

Dear Dr. Hanson,

Maddie didn't have to wait as long this time. It only took three days for the veterinarian to respond. Maddie opened the envelope, pulled out the letter, and began reading.

Dear Maddie,

A lion is not exactly what I was suggesting. A lion lives in the wild and sleeps on the ground in its den. I don't think it would tolerate braids or ponytails in that hair around its face. That hair is actually called a mane. Keeping a wild animal like a lion can be very dangerous. Have you considered a pet that lives in water?

Sincerely,
Dr. Hanson
Your concerned veterinarian

Maddie thought about Dr. Hanson's words very carefully. Although keeping a lion as a pet seemed like a great idea, Maddie agreed that a wild animal probably wouldn't be the best choice. Besides, if Alex bothered the lion too much, it might eat him. She didn't think her parents would appreciate that, so she needed to think of something else.

Maddie needed to think about pets that lived in water. She thought about the fish in the pond. She liked to watch their tails swish back and forth and she liked the little bubbles that came up from under the water.

What about an alligator? Hmmm, she thought, an alligator might also gobble up Alex. That probably wasn't the best idea. Turtles? Sharks? A whale? Maddie thought about many different animals that live in the water, but nothing seemed quite right.

Then she looked across the room and saw her backpack. That gave her another idea – a mermaid! Maddie and Chloe loved stories about mermaids, which is why both girls had pictures of mermaids on their backpacks. They loved the glistening, scaly tails and the way their bodies so gracefully popped up out of the water.

Thinking more about it, Maddie's family had a big bathtub. That would be a perfect place for the mermaid to live. Since the mermaid was part human, Maddie thought they could be the best of friends and would be able to share secrets and have tea parties. They could play dolls together and Maddie's mom could just make one extra plate of whatever she made for dinner.

Dear Dr. Hanson,
I really liked your suggestion to get an animal that lives in the water.

I have decided to get a mermaid. My mermaid could live in our bathtub and we could talk and sing whenever I'm not at school. She wouldn't be able to go for walks, but she could splash around all day in our tub. I have to thank you again for such good advice. Do you happen to know where I might be able to purchase a mermaid? I have never seen one in the stores.

Thanks for your help!

Your friend,
Maddie

She put the letter in an envelope and wrote the address on the front. She let Chloe put the stamp on the letter and they walked to the mailbox together. She slipped the letter into the mailbox and let

Chloe stand on her leg to be able to push up the red flag to let the mailman know a very important letter needed to be sent. Now she just had to wait. This time, she didn't have to wait long at all! Just two days later, she opened the mailbox to find a letter from Dr. Hanson.

Dear Maddie,

I appreciate how much thought you have put into deciding on a pet. I also love reading about mermaids. I have never actually seen one in person though and I think you would have a hard time convincing one to leave her home in the great big ocean to live in a bathtub. I know this is a difficult decision and I am glad you have asked for my help. I suggest that you visit your local pet shelter and see what pets are living there that need a good home. Keep thinking and planning, I know you will find the right pet!

Sincerely,
Dr. Hanson
Your hopeful veterinarian

Maddie read the letter a few times and sat down on the steps with a thud. Dr. Hanson was probably right. It wouldn't be fair to take such a beautiful creature from her home in the beautiful blue sea. Sadly, Maddie had no more ideas. She put her face in her hands, took a deep breath, and slid down to lay on her back on the floor. She lay on her back for a long time, trying to think. When she finally took her hands away from her face and opened her eyes, Chloe's face was right there, almost nose to nose with Maddie's.

Maddie let out a startled squeak. Alex was there too, and in his hands he held a large picture book. It was a book of animals. "We are here to help," Chloe said. Alex just nodded his head up and down. "Let's look through this book of animals and see what we can find."

For a little person, Chloe could be very smart. Maddie sat up and Chloe snuggled up to her. Alex sat on the other side. Together, they looked at all the pictures, talked about what to feed the animals, and discussed which ones might be a good fit for their family.

The kids were so busy figuring things out that they didn't hear the phone ring. Maddie's mom picked up the phone and listened carefully. "Yes, I see," she said into the phone. Maddie's mom listened for a little while longer, sometimes smiling, sometimes nodding her head. Every once in a while, she would smile and shake her head. She watched her children discuss the various animals in the book as she listened to the caller. "Of course, thank you so much for your help," Maddie's mother said before hanging up the phone.

"Maddie," she said, "is there anything you want to talk about?"

Maddie sighed. "Yes, Mom. You said I could get a pet and I have been thinking and thinking about it. I talked to my friends and I wrote letters to a veterinarian. Alex and Chloe brought me this great book about animals and we have been reading it and looking at the pictures to get ideas. I just don't know what to pick." Maddie felt tears prickling in her eyes. She tried not to let them out.

Her mom hugged her close and said, "Maddie, Dr. Hanson just called. She suggested that we go to the pet shelter. Would you like to go?"

Maddie hugged her mom tightly. "Yes Mom, thank you. Can we go right now?"

Alex and Chloe shouted "Hooray!" They closed the book, and Alex helped Chloe with her shoelaces.

Chapter 4
Pet Shelter

The kids were curious and asked many questions during the car ride. They had never been to a pet shelter before and were excited to meet some new animal friends. Maddie just knew she would find her pet finally.

After what seemed like hours, the car pulled into a parking space. As the kids piled out of the car, Maddie saw a sign that said Animal Shelter: We help pets find their forever homes. Maddie's face lit up and she looked at her mother. Her mom smiled back at her.

Maddie and her family walked into the building. Maddie's mother talked to the clerk and explained the situation.

"We are so glad you are here," the clerk said to Maddie. "Please take your time and visit with our animal friends. Let's see if you can find the pet you want. Or, just maybe a pet will find you." The clerk winked. Maddie tried to wink back but both of her eyes closed. It made the clerk chuckle.

As they walked around, they found a cage with a large greenish creature that had a long tail and scaly skin that looked dry. Maddie thought it might be a chameleon or an iguana. Maddie smiled and kept walking. Alex was fascinated. After talking to the clerk, Alex found out the animal was an iguana. He sat in front of the animal watching its tongue dart in and out of its mouth. This is better than watching TV, he thought.

In the meantime, Maddie and Chloe walked over to a small fenced area. The girls peeked over the edge of the fence and tiny sounds greeted them. Mew, Mew, Mew, the little kittens called. Chloe asked the clerk if she could pet the kittens. The clerk nodded her head.

Chloe sat next to the box and giggled as the little furry creatures wobbled around trying to get to Chloe. Maddie petted one of the little cuties, but continued to walk around. She was licked by at least five different puppies, watched a turtle climb up on a rock, and tried to keep a goat from chewing on her shirt.

Maddie sat down and folded her hands in her lap. Maddie didn't think her pet was here. She put her head down on her knees and let out all her breath in a big whoosh. Then she heard it. Looking down, Maddie noticed a hairy animal sitting right on her feet. It made little snorting sounds. It was too big to be a hamster and too hairy to be a piglet.

"I am so sorry, Miss," the clerk said. "I opened the cage to refill the water bottle for this little guinea pig here. He has been following you since he escaped. Don't worry, I'll put him back in the cage." Maddie looked at the guinea pig. She stroked his soft fur and listened to his funny little squeaky noises. She smiled, then she laughed right out loud as the guinea pig tried to climb up into her pant leg.

She knew it was right! This little guy was going home with her.

Maddie's mom filled out all the paperwork, gathered up the food and accessories, and walked the kids to the car. Alex proudly walked his iguana on a leash, Chloe held her kitten in a small box on her lap, and Maddie petted her guinea pig through its cage.

Maddie couldn't stop grinning! She couldn't wait to write the next letter to Dr. Hanson to tell her all about her new pet.

Reflection

Dear reader,

I love animals and have always wanted a pet of my own. I just couldn't decide what the right pet might be. I looked at all the pets in my neighborhood and I did a lot of thinking. I came up with some great ideas! However, I learned that I needed to know about each animals' needs to make the right choice. It was a really tough decision. But I realized that I could count on my friends, my family, and an even a pet expert to help me make the best choice. I couldn't be happier with my new pet!

Love,
Maddie

Discussion Questions

1. What steps does Maddie take to try to make a decision about getting a pet?

2. Why was it important for the author to use dialogue?

3. How does Chloe help Maddie with her problem?

4. Why is a veterinarian a good choice to help Maddie?

5. How would you describe the pet shelter?

Vocabulary

Make a hopscotch board using chalk on the sidewalk or by writing these vocabulary words on paper and spreading them on the floor. As you hop from one word to another, say the name of the word, tell what it means, and use it in a sentence.

consult
occasion
pounced
professional
shelter
squatted
suggested
veterinarian

Writing Prompt

Do you remember a time when you had to make a difficult decision? Write about the problem you faced and how you decided what to do.

Q & A with Author Kelli Hicks

Do you have any pets?

I am a dog lover and right now I have two dogs. Gingerbread is my golden retriever. She is sweet, gentle, and loving. I am not sure what Emma June is, but she is highly energetic and needs lots of exercise. She likes to eat things that don't belong to her if she doesn't get enough exercise.

Are you like Maddie in the story?

Maddie loves all pets and would probably own a zoo if she could. I know about caring for dogs and definitely would have more of them if I had a bigger house. Maddie has a brother and sister who she loves, but can find difficult to be around. So do I! But, I think that both Maddie and I love and appreciate our siblings. Life wouldn't be the same without them.

What do you do if you have a difficult problem to solve?

Problems pop up in our lives every day. First, I try to stay calm. Then, I try to come up with as many solutions as I can think of. Sometimes my choice works out great and sometimes it doesn't. Either way, I know that I make my own choices and that I can't blame anyone else for the decisions I make. If the choice doesn't work out, I try again.

Connections

Do you want to help? Animal shelters provide love and care to all kinds of animals. You can help! Contact your local shelter to see what they need. Collect blankets, toys, or food to donate to the shelter. Let your friends and family know about shelters and encourage them to help as well.

Websites to Visit

Check out this list of animal sites:
www.kidsites.com/sites-edu/animals.htm

Learn how you can help shelter animals:
http://petnewsandviews.com/2012/10/10-ways-children-can-help-animal-shelters

Fun facts about pets and pet owners:
http://pbskids.org/itsmylife/family/pets/article2

About the Author

Kelli Hicks is a teacher
and dog lover who lives
with her family in Tampa,
Florida. When she is not
teaching or writing, she
can usually be found
cleaning up whatever her
dog Emma June has decided to tear up.
She loves to be at the soccer field watching
her son and daughter play soccer.

About the Illustrator

My name is Tatio Viana. I was born, raised, and still live in Madrid. In order to do something "serious" while drawing, I studied advertising and actually worked as an advertising Art Director for many years, until in one of those famous mergers I was unemployed. So I dared to try what I love: illustrating. I have said "dare" because I am a self taught illustrator. I learned filling a lot of bins and enjoying the work of the thousands of illustrators I love.